A Deadly Obsession

by
Anne Schraff

Perfection Learning Corporation
Logan, Iowa 51546

Cover Illustration: Michael Aspengren

© 1997 by Perfection Learning Corporation,
1000 North Second Avenue, P.O. Box 500,
Logan, Iowa 51546-1099.
ISBN 0-7891-1965-X Paperback
ISBN 0-7807-6611-3 Cover Craft®
Printed in the U.S.A.
11 12 13 14 15 16 17 18 19 20 PP 08 07 06 05

1 "SO WHAT DO you want to do tonight?" Summer Jackson leaned against her locker and smiled up at her boyfriend, Rashad Gaines. Rashad towered over her like he towered over almost everyone at East High. At seventeen, he stood almost six foot four, with long, muscular arms and legs. Of East Indian heritage, Rashad had warm bronze skin that glowed with good health and energy.

Rashad grinned down at her. "Oh, I've got a great idea for tonight, baby," he said. "Want to come with me and help clean up the Palace Theater?"

"You're going to clean up the old Palace Theater?" Summer asked, wide-eyed with surprise.

"Sure," Rashad said. "What's the big deal? I'm saving for a new car, and Mrs. Robinson is paying good money. Why don't you come along? It'll be fun."

Mrs. Robinson was an elderly widow who wanted to sell the theater she and her late husband had owned for years. She had asked Rashad to clean it up before the realtors walked through it.

Summer shook her head firmly, her dark ponytail dancing around her shoulders. "No way, Rashad. A million dollars wouldn't tempt me to set foot in that place." She lowered her voice. "People say it's haunted."

Rashad threw back his head and laughed. "Summer, you've been reading too many Stephen King books!"

Summer looked slightly offended. "Well, it's true," she protested. "People say that the ghosts of actors who once performed at the Palace still haunt the place. Nobody I know will go near it." She shook her head again. "Nope, I'm not going, and I wish you wouldn't either."

Rashad put an arm around her shoulders and gave her a squeeze. "Now, don't worry about me. I'm tougher than any ghost. Tell you what. After Mrs. Robinson pays me, I'll take you to dinner—any place you want, okay?"

Summer smiled. "Trying to bribe me, huh?" she asked, giving in. "All right,

Rashad. Go on and do your janitor act. But be careful. Even if there aren't any ghosts, that building is pretty run-down. Just don't fall through any holes in the floor, okay?"

"Don't worry, I'll be careful," Rashad promised. "Call you later tonight, okay?"

Rashad waved to Summer as he hoisted his book bag onto his shoulder. He turned and headed down the hall to the front doors.

Once outside, Rashad could feel the warm autumn sun on his face. The front steps and sidewalk of East High were crowded with students, all relieved to be out of class for yet another day. Rashad headed toward the student parking lot.

"Hey, Rashad, wait up!"

Rashad turned. His best friend Franklin came running up behind him. "I tried to catch you before you left, man, but you weren't at your locker. Where were you?"

Rashad grinned. "Hanging out by Summer's locker."

Franklin grinned back. "I should have figured. So I guess shooting hoops is out of the question, huh? You're probably heading home to get dressed for a hot date tonight."

" 'Fraid not," Rashad said, shaking his head. "I'm working tonight. I'm on my way to clean up the Palace Theater right now. The owner hired me. She wants to sell the place. Want to come along? There's probably enough work for both of us."

Franklin stared at his friend. "You're yanking my chain, right?" he said. "You're not really going to mess around in that old place, are you?"

"Oh no, not you too," Rashad groaned. "I already got this lecture from Summer. Ghosts, goblins, and things that go bump in the night, all lurking in the shadows of the Palace Theater. Give me a break."

Franklin looked serious. "You should listen to your lady, Rash. There's been some strange rumors about that place for years."

"It's in the middle of downtown, for crying out loud!" Rashad scoffed. "Most of the people who hang out in that area are winos. They'd see strange things in Mister Roger's neighborhood. Hey, I've got to get going. You coming along or not?"

Franklin shook his head.

"Okay, then I'll see you tomorrow," Rashad said, unlocking his car door.

"Yeah," Franklin replied. Then under his breath, he added, "I hope so, man."

Rashad drove downtown and found a parking space not far from the theater. Originally, the Palace had been a movie house, showing everything from Charlie Chaplin movies to *Gone With the Wind*. It was later remodeled as a playhouse. But the Palace had closed its doors more than twenty-five years ago. Since then, its only patrons had been rats, spiders, and an occasional vandal.

Rashad parked his car in front of the theater and got out. He paused for a moment to study the building. It had once been one of the classiest on the block. An enormous granite structure, it was decorated with elaborate carvings. A huge marquee still stretched out over the sidewalk, but most of the light bulbs were missing or broken. It had been a long time since the theater had lit up the night sky.

Rashad reached into his pocket and pulled out the key Mrs. Robinson had given him. He unlocked the big double doors and stepped inside. He spotted a light switch by the entrance and flicked it on. A few of the bulbs in the huge chandelier hanging above the lobby came to life, casting an odd glow. But Rashad sighed with relief. Mrs. Robinson had kept her promise to have the electricity turned back on. He stepped into the lobby and looked around.

"Whew!" he whistled as he gazed around the room. "No wonder Mrs. Robinson's paying such good money!"

The lobby looked like a dumpster had exploded. Piles of posters from old movies and plays littered the marble floor, and grimy layers of dust coated every surface. An ancient popcorn machine stood behind the refreshment counter, its glass sides splattered with old butter. Glancing up again, Rashad noticed thick swags of cobwebs hanging from the old chandelier.

"Man!" Rashad said. "Smells musty in here."

Rashad bent down and began gathering up the posters. He noticed that most of them were from movies shown in the 1930s and '40s. There were posters of stars like Humphrey Bogart, James Cagney, Greta Garbo, and Bette Davis. Rashad carried them over to the refreshment counter and laid them down, smoothing out several for a better look.

As Rashad stood looking at the posters, he heard a soft rustling noise, like rats scurrying around. In spite of himself, Rashad felt the hair on the back of his neck rise.

Should've brought my cat, Rashad joked to himself. He'd laughed at Summer's fears about this place, but he had to admit, it *was* sort of creepy.

Come on, man, he scolded himself, don't be a fool. Even Vanessa said she wouldn't be afraid to come here for a nice piece of change. Of course, Vanessa's pretty cool, he admitted. She's as tough as they come. He chuckled, thinking about his sister. Maybe I should have brought *her*, he thought.

Rashad left the posters on the counter and got back to work. Suddenly he heard a crashing noise somewhere in the building.

"Huh?" Rashad said aloud. Is someone else here? he wondered.

"Hey! Who's there?" Rashad shouted. Silence. He shrugged and returned to his work.

Rashad bent down and picked up another rolled-up poster. He worked it open and saw the face of a handsome, intense man glaring at him. Rashad shivered slightly. The man was dressed in a white lab coat, the kind a scientist might wear. His eyes seemed to reflect the red background of the poster. In fact, the eyes almost glowed. The title on the poster was *A Deadly Obsession.* Rashad scanned the poster. In small letters at the bottom, it read "Now at the Palace Theater, October 20–31, 1970."

"Wow," Rashad whispered to himself, "I'll bet this was one of the last plays ever performed here. Maybe the very last one." He studied the actor's face again. "I'm not surprised the Palace closed," he said to the picture. "You're one mean-looking dude. *I* wouldn't pay money to see you, that's for sure." He put the poster on the refreshment counter with the others.

Rashad worked for almost two hours. In all that time, he only managed to clear a path through the lobby. He had created a huge pile of junk to haul to the dumpster out back. Finally, he stopped and stretched. Looking around, Rashad spotted the double doors that led into the auditorium. I'd better take a look and see how bad it is in there, he thought. I may have to borrow a semi to get all this junk out of here!

Rashad crossed the marble floor of the lobby. His footsteps echoed off the high ceiling. As he reached the doors, he paused. From inside the auditorium, he could hear scurrying noises again. Gotta be rats, he thought. Well, it's going to take more than rats to scare me away. Easing open the double doors, he slipped into the auditorium and looked around.

Rows of old red velvet chairs filled the room, each one sporting its own layer of dust. Matching red velvet curtains sagged on either side of the old stage. The stage itself was cluttered with furniture, boxes, and what looked like old stage props and backdrops.

Rashad walked down the center aisle and approached the steps leading up to the stage. Suddenly he caught a movement out of the corner of his eye, as if one of the curtains had swayed for just an instant.

Rashad stopped and looked around. "Is anybody there?" he called. His voice echoed through the silence of the great room. The curtain hung limp alongside the stage.

Must have imagined it, Rashad thought as he climbed the steps to the stage. Still, I'd better keep my eyes open. Some homeless person might have broken in and taken refuge here. Probably not dangerous, but you never know.

Once on the stage, Rashad surveyed the clutter. One prop was a section of white picket fence. He smiled and wondered if it had been used for a production of *Tom Sawyer*.

But as Rashad glanced around, his smile was replaced by a puzzled frown. A few feet away sat one of the strangest things he'd ever seen on a stage—a tall glass box with a myriad of wires coming out of it. Inside the box was a high-backed chair with more wires extending down the sides. Looks like a cross between a telephone booth and an electric chair, Rashad thought. Curious, he moved closer.

I wonder what this was used for? he mused. He was reaching out to touch the contraption when he noticed something. That's weird, he thought. There's no dust on it. He ran his fingers across the glass to make sure. But unlike everything else in the theater, the glass box was immaculate.

Suddenly the lights went out, and Rashad was standing in total darkness.

"What the—" Rashad said aloud. He felt a cold draft on the back of his neck. He started to turn but never had the chance. Wham! Something heavy hit him on top of his head. Rashad staggered and fell, landing face down and unconscious on the dust-covered stage.

2 RASHAD GROANED AND tried to open his eyes. His head throbbed, and even moving his eyelids hurt. He was still lying on the stage, but now he was on his back. Barely opening his eyes, he saw that some of the stage lights overhead were on. They cast an odd blue light onto the stage. At least the power's back on, he thought.

He tried to use his hands to help himself sit up but couldn't. Raising his head off the floor, he saw that his hands were tied together with some kind of thin, strong rope. He tried to get to his feet and discovered that his ankles were roped together too. He felt like a calf at a rodeo.

"Help!" Rashad yelled. He winced as arrows of pain zinged through his head. "Somebody help me!" Everything was quiet.

Rashad let his head drop back to the floor. There was no one to hear him, he realized. That is, no one except maybe the person who'd hit him and tied him up.

Rashad inched along the floor of the stage, his eyes growing a little more accustomed to the strange light. He felt cold terror. Had he stumbled onto a criminal's lair? he wondered. Chills crawled up his spine. What was going on here that would cause someone to attack him and tie him up?

Somebody was coming! Rashad heard a determined step. The blurry figure of a tall but slightly stooped man appeared in the dark recesses of the stage.

"Hey, what's going on?" Rashad cried. "Who are you? What do you want?"

The man moved a little closer but not close enough for Rashad to get a good look at him. "Perfect!" Rashad heard him say.

Rashad was confused. "Perfect?" he asked. "What's perfect? What are you talking about?"

"*You*, my boy, are perfect," said the man. "Absolutely perfect!"

"Perfect for what?" demanded Rashad. "I'm just the guy Mrs. Robinson hired to clean up this place."

The man chuckled. "Oh, you'll know soon enough," he said. He turned to the side and seemed to be addressing someone nearby. "All right," he ordered. "Get busy."

From out of the shadows, Rashad saw a large figure appear. Suddenly Rashad heard the auditorium door slam. "Hey, Rash! You in here?" a voice called. Rashad gasped in relief. It was Franklin.

"Franklin! Run, man! Get the cops!" Rashad yelled at the top of his lungs. Franklin did an about-face and ran out of the building.

"You fool!" the old man hissed at Rashad. "You don't know what you're doing!" He turned to the other figure. "Let's get out of here," he said. But as they turned to go, the man said to Rashad, "I'll see you again." Then they were gone.

Franklin didn't waste any time. In a matter of minutes, Rashad heard sirens. Two police officers burst into the auditorium with Franklin at their heels. The officers were carrying powerful flashlights. "Rashad! Where are you?" Franklin yelled.

"Here! On the stage! I'm tied up!" Rashad yelled back.

Franklin and the officers ran down the aisle and onto the stage. A few minutes later, Rashad was free. He sat up slowly, still dizzy from the bump on his head. One of the police officers reached out and grabbed his arm.

"Easy, son," she said. "I'm Officer Bates. Can you tell us what happened?"

Rashad explained about being hit over the head and then waking up with his hands and ankles bound.

"Did you see anyone?" asked the other officer.

"Yeah, a couple of guys. One was older. The other was a big guy. But I didn't get a look at their faces. It was too dark."

Officer Bates nodded. "Probably just some weirdos sleeping here," she said, glancing around. "It's a pretty easy building to get into." She frowned as she looked at Rashad. "Are you sure you're okay?"

"Yeah, I'm fine," said Rashad, standing up. "I just need to get my bearings for a second."

After a few more questions, the police told Rashad he could go home. "We'll notify the owner of the building," said one of the officers. "And if we turn up anything, we'll be in touch."

"I'll walk you to your car, Rashad," said Franklin. "Mine's parked right in front of it."

"Thanks," Rashad replied.

On the way through the lobby, Franklin said, "Man, I told you something bad would happen in this place."

"Come on, Franklin," Rashad protested. "You heard the police officer. It was just a crazy fluke." He shook his head. "Just my luck. I get a good job cleaning up the Palace, and I run into a couple of nuts."

Franklin frowned, and his dark eyes narrowed. "Rashad, maybe it was no fluke," he said with worry in his voice. "Maybe it's something more than that."

"Like what?" Rashad demanded.

"Well, I didn't tell you earlier, but my mom used to work at the Palace Theater a long time ago," Franklin said, "and she told me some weird things about it."

The two boys paused while Rashad fished the key out of his pocket. "Don't tell me," Rashad said, locking the doors to the theater. "All kinds of dead actors haunt the place, right?"

"No, see, the last play they had there—it was called *A Deadly Obsession*," Franklin said.

"Yeah, I know. I saw the poster," said Rashad impatiently. "So what?"

"Well, my mom said the play was about this mad scientist who didn't like getting old, see? So he built this contraption, some kind of youth machine. Then he'd lure some young guy into it, juice it up, and the old guy would be young again," Franklin said.

Rashad laughed out loud. "Yeah? And what happened to the kid?" he asked.

Franklin's face became serious. "He was history, if you know what I mean."

"Oh, Franklin, that's crazy," Rashad said. "It was just a play. You don't really believe something like that would work, do you?"

"*I* don't believe it," said Franklin. "But let's say some crazy guy out there *does*. Let's say he's looking for a young guy in real good physical condition. That's you, for sure."

"Oh, man, this is getting wilder by the minute," Rashad said, laughing again.

"Maybe so," Franklin replied. "But if I were you, I'd be avoiding that place like the plague. That old dude might just be waiting for someone to stumble into his trap."

Rashad looked doubtfully at his friend.

"I'm not joking, man," Franklin said. "There are a lot of sick people out there. And there's been a rumor on the street. According to a lot of people, you wouldn't be the first guy to die at the Palace."

Suddenly Rashad realized just how serious his friend was. But this is crazy, he thought. There's no way something like this could be happening—especially to me. Rashad shook off a shiver. Besides, I need that money, he reminded himself. If I add it to what I've already saved, I'll have just enough to buy a newer car. Am I ready to turn my back on all that cash?

The two friends reached Rashad's car.

"Hey, thanks for rescuing me tonight, man," Rashad said, opening the car door.

"No problem," said Franklin. "Summer was worried and called me."

Rashad climbed into his car. "And thanks for the warning," he said. "I'll think about what you said."

"I hope so," said Franklin. "I hope you'll think real hard. I'll wait here 'til you get your car started."

Rashad started his engine. As usual, he had to wait while it clanked and sputtered before he could take off.

"Listen to that," he called out the window to Franklin. "Do I need a different car or what?"

"Depends on how much you're willing to spend for it," Franklin replied.

"What do you mean?" asked Rashad.

"No car is worth your life, man," said Franklin.

3 AT DINNER THAT evening, Rashad told his family what had happened at the Palace.

"Rashad!" cried his mother, jumping up to inspect his head. "Are you all right?"

"Oh, Mom," said Rashad, "I'm fine. It was just a bump on the head."

"Just a bump on the head? Why didn't the police call us?" she demanded, parting his hair with her fingers for a closer look.

"I told them I was fine," Rashad said, leaning away from his mother. He didn't want her fussing over him. "They think it was probably just some weirdos sleeping at the Palace. No big deal."

Mr. Gaines frowned. "Well, Rashad, I'll tell you one thing. You're not going back to that place. It's too dangerous."

"Your father's right," agreed Mrs. Gaines. "I didn't particularly want you going there in the first place."

"Why, Mom?" Vanessa wanted to know.

"I saw a play there years ago. *A Deadly*

Obsession, I think it was called." She shook her head. "Such a strange little piece. And such a strange man who played the lead. I remember feeling real spooky as I watched it—almost as if there were true evil in the theater. It was as though at any time, something could sneak up behind you in that dark place and grab you."

"Creepy!" said Vanessa. "Hey, Rashad, maybe it was the ghost of that old actor that hit you!"

"Don't be ridiculous, Vanessa," Rashad said. He turned back to his father. "Dad," he continued, "whoever attacked me is probably long gone by now. And I really need that money. You know how bad my car is."

"Your car's fine," replied his dad. "It just needs a little tune-up. I'll help you with it this weekend."

"But I hate to let Mrs. Robinson down," Rashad went on. "She's depending on me."

Mr. Gaines laid down his fork. "Mrs. Robinson will just have to find someone else. If she's smart, she'll hire a professional cleaning crew. You're not to go back there again, Rashad, and that's final."

Rashad sighed. He knew that to continue arguing would be futile. "All right, Dad." He shook his head sadly, thinking of how close he'd come to getting a new car.

* * *

Summer was waiting for him at his locker when Rashad got to school the next day.

"Rashad, are you okay?" she asked anxiously.

"I'm fine, Summer," he assured her. "You know my head's too hard for anyone to break with just one thump." He smiled at his girlfriend. "But it's a lucky thing you got nervous and called Franklin. He showed up just in time."

Summer shivered. "I knew there was something creepy about that place."

"The only thing creepy about the Palace is the people who hang out there," Rashad answered. "But you can relax. My dad laid down the law. I won't be going back there again."

Summer looked relieved. "Thank goodness," she said.

Rashad went to his classes and tried to forget all about the Palace Theater. But after school, curiosity got the best of him, and he went to the school library.

"Ms. Wallace," he asked the librarian, "do you think you'd have a copy of a play called *A Deadly Obsession?* It was performed at the old Palace Theater a long time ago."

Ms. Wallace smiled. "Oh, I remember that play, Rashad. It was all the rage a few years ago. I believe it was written by a man named Arthur Van Horn. He was a science fiction writer. Would you like to check out a copy of it?"

"Um, I guess so," Rashad said, though it made him feel a little uneasy.

Ms. Wallace disappeared into the stacks for a minute. "Here you go," she said when she returned.

"Thanks," said Rashad, giving her his library card and quickly stuffing the play into his book bag. He didn't want Summer or Franklin to see the book. They might get the idea that he actually believed their claims about the Palace.

After dinner that evening, Rashad went to his room to do homework. As he dug through his book bag, he saw the play. Might as well read this first, he thought. But before he could start, his mother called, "Rashad, will you take Lucky for a walk?"

"Sure, Mom," Rashad said, laying the play aside. I'll get back to it later, he thought.

Rashad was at the corner of his street when a stranger called to him. "Young fellow!"

Rashad turned to see a nicely dressed man wearing glasses. He was tall with narrow shoulders and a square face. "Can you tell me the location of the nearest deli?" he inquired amiably.

"Just down the block to the first cross street," Rashad answered.

"Thank you," the man said. "You're very kind." He turned to go but then turned back. "Say, I'm afraid my eyes aren't too good. Would you be able to come along and show me?"

Rashad shrugged. He started to take a step toward the man, but then he stopped. There was something about the man's eyes—something scary. For a terrible moment Rashad felt like he was looking into the face of the man pictured on the play poster. His instincts told him to run away. "You can't miss the deli," he mumbled as he pointed down the street. Then Rashad pulled on Lucky's leash and quickly turned in the opposite direction and hurried home.

As Rashad neared his house, he felt silly. What a fool I am, he thought. I've let this thing spook me. I refused to do a favor for a poor old guy because I'm letting this crazy business get to me!

Rashad went back to his room and opened the play. It was poorly written and filled with flowery, old-fashioned language, but the climactic scene gripped Rashad.

The scientist's lines read, "I am growing old and weak. My comely appearance fades. My wisdom wanes! But the scientific genius of my mind has led me to develop this splendid machine. Some fair youth I shall draw into the machine. And as he weakens and then perishes, I shall grow strong and splendid once again!"

Rashad could almost hear the exaggerated and overly dramatic tone of the actor's voice.

"Hey, Rashad," Vanessa cried, bursting into his room. "What are you reading?"

"Nothing," Rashad said, stuffing the play into his bag. But Vanessa sprang at him, snatching the book away.

"Oh, man," she said, "you got a copy of that dumb play Mom was talking about. Rashad, this is science fiction stuff. I mean, you can't make an old dude young again with a machine."

"Give me that, Vanessa," Rashad demanded, reaching for the play. "*I* know it's not possible, but what if someone else thinks it is? Don't you think there are plenty of people out there who'd believe something like this?"

"Rashad," Vanessa said, plunking herself down on the edge of the bed, "why don't you just find out if that actor dude is still alive?"

"And just how am I supposed to do that?" Rashad wanted to know. Then he remembered. "Wait a minute," he said. "When I was at the theater, I saw a poster advertising that play. I wonder if his name is on it."

"There's only one way to find out," Vanessa said.

"What do you mean?" asked Rashad cautiously. He could tell his sister was about to say something he didn't want to hear.

Vanessa lowered her voice. "Sneak back into the theater real quick and find out his name," she said.

"But Dad told me to stay away from that place," Rashad reminded her.

"I know, Rashad. But the police checked the place out. Like you said, the guy who hit you is probably long gone. If you play your cards right, Dad'll never know."

Rashad thought a moment. "Boy, I'd really like to," he said. "This business is getting on my nerves, and I'd like to put my mind at ease." He thought a moment. "I do still have the key," he said. "And maybe I can get Franklin to go with me tomorrow. All right, Vanessa, I'll do it!"

4 AFTER ALGEBRA THE next day, Rashad caught up with Franklin. "Hey, Franklin," he said, "how about coming with me to the Palace Theater after school today?"

Franklin looked at Rashad like he was crazy. "No way, man!" he said. "You just about got yourself killed the last time you were there."

"Hey, the police went over the place with a fine-tooth comb," Rashad said. "I think it's safe now. Besides, I've got to go. I need to find out the name of the guy who starred in that play you told me about."

"Why?" Franklin wanted to know.

"I want to check to see if he's still alive—you know, set my mind at ease."

Franklin hesitated, and then said, "All right. I'll go. *Someone's* got to keep an eye on you."

After school, the two boys drove to the Palace. On the way, Rashad decided to tell Franklin about reading *A Deadly*

Obsession the night before.

"You were right, Franklin," Rashad said. "The old dude pushed the young guy into an electrical box, and the poor kid was history." Rashad saw his friend shudder.

"Sounds like something that would make a good horror flick," commented Franklin.

"Yeah," Rashad said, pausing at the door of the theater. Now that he was there, he found that he was reluctant to go in. Some of the fear he had felt the other night surged within him.

"Come on, Rash, let's get this over with," Franklin said, looking around nervously.

Rashad unlocked the door and headed right for the refreshment counter with Franklin close behind. He found the poster from *A Deadly Obsession*. "Look, here it is," he said, unrolling it. Again the face of the actor in the white lab coat glared out at him.

"Man, that is one evil-looking dude," said Franklin.

"Well, this is only a drawing of him. I suppose he was made to look as weird as possible to draw people in to see the play," Rashad said. He scanned the poster quickly. "Let's see, here's his name— Spencer Hoover. That's what I wanted."

"Good. Now let's get out of here," Franklin said. "This place is like a tomb. It gives me the creeps."

"Yeah, me too," Rashad agreed, rolling up the poster and tucking it under his arm.

"You taking that creepy thing with you?" asked Franklin in disbelief.

Rashad shrugged. "Why not?" he said. "Nobody else wants it, and it might come in handy."

As the two boys headed for the doors, Rashad stopped. "Wait a minute!" he said, snapping his fingers.

"What now?" asked Franklin.

"The theater office is down that hallway. I remember seeing it when I was cleaning. I wonder if they kept files on the actors who starred in the plays here. Let's go check it out."

"Oh, man," Franklin groaned. "Do we have to?"

"We might as well, as long as we're

here," Rashad said. "Look, Franklin, I don't like being here either, but I've got to find out about that guy Hoover. Don't back out on me now."

"All right," said Franklin, "but let's make this quick."

Rashad and Franklin entered the office and looked around. On one end was a roll-top desk and an old chair on casters. On the other were three file cabinets.

"Over here," said Rashad. "Look. These drawers have labels on them. Let's see. Actors, A through C . . . Actors, D through F . . . here it is—Actors, G through I. If there's a file on Hoover, it ought to be in this drawer."

Rashad opened the drawer and began leafing through the files.

"Hurry up, man," said Franklin, glancing around nervously.

"I'm trying," said Rashad. "Bingo! Hoover, Spencer." He took the folder on Hoover out of the file and tucked it under his arm with the poster.

"You taking *that* with you too?" asked Franklin.

"Well, let me ask you this," said Rashad.

"Do you want to sit here while I leisurely read through the whole thing?"

"No way!" said Franklin. "You can bring it back later. Let's get out of here."

When Rashad got home, Vanessa was waiting for him. "Did you get the guy's name, Rash?" she asked excitedly.

"Yeah. It's Spencer Hoover," Rashad said. "Let's go up to my room, and I'll show you what I've got."

Upstairs, Rashad spread out the play poster on his bed. "Look," he said.

"That's him?" Vanessa cried. "Wow. He *is* scary!"

"Yeah," agreed Rashad. "Now look at this." He showed her the folder.

"What is it?" asked Vanessa.

"I think it's like a personnel file. Let's open it and see." He opened the folder and pulled out the first sheet of paper.

"That looks like a biography," said Vanessa.

"Yeah, it does," Rashad agreed. "They print short biographies of the actors on play programs. Let's see, looks like he did a couple of movies early in his career. And he was twenty-nine when he was in that

play, so I guess he'd be in his fifties now."
He picked up the next page.

"I'll bet this is a contract," Rashad said.
"Yep, it's for *A Deadly Obsession*. Look,
it's signed down here." At the bottom of
the page was scrawled "Spencer Hoover."

"Hey, look, there's his agent's name."
Vanessa said, pointing at a line on the
page. "Agent: Camille Morrison,
Hollywood, California. I'll bet she'd know
what happened to him."

"Probably so," agreed Rashad. "But I
don't think Mom and Dad would appreci-
ate a phone call to Hollywood on their
bill."

"Leave it to me, big brother," said
Vanessa, smiling slyly. "You found out the
guy's name. I'll find out if he's dead or
alive."

Rashad shrugged. "Be my guest," he
said. "I've had enough of playing detec-
tive, for awhile, anyway."

"All right!" said Vanessa gleefully. She
took the contract and headed toward her
own room down the hall. After she'd gone,
Rashad thought about Spencer Hoover. If
he was only in his fifties, there was a good

chance he was still alive. The thought sent a shiver down his spine.

The phone rang around ten that night. Rashad picked it up in his room.

"Hey, Gaines, you still alive?" came a familiar, husky voice on the other end of the line. It was a voice Rashad didn't want to hear. Quincy Martin was an old class-mate . . . an old nightmare. He was big and mean, and he'd made Rashad's life miser-able in middle school. Rashad would never forget his pain and humiliation in sixth and seventh grades when Quincy was the biggest kid in class. He would cor-ner Rashad and the other smaller kids and demand their lunch money. The price of refusing him was a brutal kidney punch when the teacher wasn't looking.

Quincy had started high school with his class but dropped out in the tenth grade. By then Rashad had grown as tall as Quincy, although he didn't weigh as much, and he couldn't be bullied quite so easily. In fact, one time Rashad had embarrassed Quincy in front of the entire physical edu-cation class. Rashad had caught Quincy off guard and pinned him during the wrestling unit. He knew Quincy had never forgiven him for that.

"What rock did you crawl out from under, Martin?" Rashad asked. "I thought you'd be doing hard time by now."

"Just wanted to let you know I heard it on the street that you're dead meat, Gaines," Quincy said.

"What are you talking about?" Rashad asked, trying to keep his voice from shaking. "You having bad dreams or something?"

"You wish, man. Somebody's fixing to put you in the ground, man. You interested in hearing more about it?" Quincy asked.

Rashad's mind spun. The only people who knew about what happened at the Palace Theater were his family and friends. They wouldn't have told Quincy. So where was he picking up the bad news?

"Meet me at the corner of Fifth and Oak in fifteen minutes," Quincy said, "and I'll tell you all about it."

"You're crazier than I thought, Martin," Rashad shot back. "You think I'd meet you *anywhere?*"

"Your choice, man," Quincy replied. "But I'm selling good information. Might save your neck—or aren't you interested in staying alive?"

Before Rashad could answer, Quincy hung up.

Was Quincy really going to be waiting at Fifth and Oak? Rashad wondered. And for what? To bust my head?

Rashad tried to figure out where Quincy Martin fit into the picture. Was the whole thing at the Palace Quincy's doing? Or did Quincy have some connection with the old actor?

Rashad had no intention of going to Fifth and Oak to find out what Quincy was up to. Whatever it was, he knew that meeting Quincy on a dark street was just asking for trouble.

Suddenly Rashad remembered that his Aunt Leslie lived on Fifth Street. She could see the intersection of Fifth and Oak from her upstairs window. And Rashad could get to Aunt Leslie's down some alleys without ever getting near that intersection.

Rashad left his home and sprinted over to his Aunt Leslie's.

"What a nice surprise," Aunt Leslie said when Rashad arrived. "But it's pretty late, honey."

"I got kind of a problem, Aunt Les," Rashad explained. "Some guy asked me to meet him tonight at Fifth and Oak, but I'm not sure why. I want to look out your window and see what he's up to."

Aunt Leslie looked dubious. "You're not in some kind of trouble, are you, Rashad?"

"No, Aunt Les, I'm fine," Rashad replied. "Really."

Before his aunt could say more, Rashad ran upstairs to the corner bedroom. He purposely left the light off so that he could see out, but no one could see in. He looked down into the street. Sure enough, there was Quincy Martin looking bigger and meaner than Rashad had remembered. He stood in the filmy glow of a street lamp. Parked at the curb was his battered green van. Quincy leaned against the lamp, glancing up and down the street from time to time. He really thinks I'm crazy enough to show up, Rashad thought, shaking his head.

Rashad took a second look at the van. A man was sitting in the passenger seat. Rashad couldn't see the man's face until he lit a cigarette. Then the brief glow of the match lit up his features just long enough for Rashad to see that the man had dark glasses and a squarish face. Rashad felt an icy finger of fear creep up his spine. It was the same man who'd asked for directions to the deli the other night! And probably the same man from the Palace Theater.

Sweat popped out in beads on Rashad's body. They were working together— Quincy and the man. Quincy and Spencer Hoover? Rashad wondered. Quincy and the madman? Rashad turned away from the window.

"Honey, you look like you've seen a ghost," Aunt Leslie whispered. She had entered the room without Rashad knowing it. Now she touched his arm gently. "You okay?" she asked.

No, Rashad thought to himself. Not okay. Not okay at all. But he forced a thin smile and told his aunt he was fine.

5 AUNT LESLIE LOOKED out the window. "That boy down there," she said. "That's the Martin boy, isn't it? He's a bad one. Always has been. His parents just let him run wild. Why's he just standing there? Should I call the police, Rashad?"

"And tell them what?" Rashad asked wearily. He could imagine the look on the police officer's face when he told him his story—a demented actor who believes he can recapture his youth by stuffing a kid into an electrified telephone booth. It would be like saying Dr. Frankenstein was back and was building his monster in Rashad's basement. Yeah, right!

A few minutes later, Rashad and Aunt Leslie watched as Quincy left the street corner, jumped into the van, and drove away. Rashad gave his aunt a quick hug and headed down the stairs to the street. He stood for a moment at Fifth and Oak, looking around for any clues. But the corner was empty now with nothing but a cat yowling from atop its perch on a garbage can nearby.

Rashad headed home the normal way, thinking he was in the clear. He'd gotten only a few blocks down Oak when suddenly he saw two headlights approaching. It was the green van. Quincy was cruising the neighborhood, just in case Rashad showed up. The van was heading toward Rashad!

"Oh, man," Rashad groaned, "why didn't I take the back way?" He looked around. Most of the stores were closed now. There was no chance of running into a well-lit deli. Rashad knew his best bet was to sprint down the sidewalk, turn at Main, and jog right into the police station. But as Rashad broke into a run, the van sped up and quickly overtook him. Quincy turned his wheel sharply, almost climbing the curb and smashing Rashad against a fence. The van was so close now that Rashad could hear Quincy and the old man talking.

"Careful!" rasped the man. He obviously didn't want Rashad dead.

Sweat streamed down Rashad's body as he turned and started running down Main. Quincy stopped the van and leaped out, his huge arms almost bursting the seams of his T-shirt. He had a rope slung over one shoulder and a nasty grin on his face. He was enjoying his role as the hunter, and Rashad was his prey.

"Gonna getcha, fool," Quincy yelled at Rashad. It was what he used to say years ago when Rashad, a skinny twelve-year-old, would walk home from middle school. And more often than not, Quincy got him. Rashad had come home with black eyes and a bloody nose more than once.

Now Rashad stared straight ahead as he ran. His heart felt like a hot stone in his chest. His arms ached. He felt like he was dying. Only a few more blocks to the police station, but could he make it?

"Gaining on you, fool," Quincy laughed, pounding closer. He sounded so close that Rashad was afraid to glance back for fear it would slow him down.

Rashad decided to take a shortcut through a parking lot. He knew that the parking lot was surrounded on three sides by a low fence. When he was on the track team, Rashad had cleared barriers like that with ease. Whispering a desperate prayer, Rashad leaped the fence successfully. Quincy did not do as well. He was heavier and clumsier. His struggle to get over the fence allowed Rashad a few precious seconds to race ahead and clamber up the steps of the police station.

"You ain't getting away, Gaines," Quincy screamed into the darkness. But by that time, Rashad was on his way through the big double doors.

I'll ask for Officer Bates, Rashad decided as he approached the front desk where a young man in a blue uniform sat. He was working on a stack of paperwork. As Rashad approached, the officer looked up and smiled. "Can I help you?" he asked.

"Um . . . yes. I'd like to talk to Officer Bates," Rashad said nervously.

"I'm sorry," the young man answered. "Officer Bates is off duty tonight. But if you can tell me what this is about, I'll get another officer to help you."

Rashad quickly gave the officer his name. Then he blurted out that he'd been attacked two days before, and that someone was still stalking him.

"I'll ask Officer Watkins to speak with you," said the officer. He gestured toward a bench along one wall. "If you'll just have a seat, I'll page him."

Rashad sat down and fidgeted for a few minutes. Before long, a policeman came down the hall and walked up to him. He was short and red-faced. His uniform shirt strained at every button.

"I'm Officer Watkins," he said, offering his hand.

Rashad stood up and shook the man's hand. "I'm Rashad Gaines," he said.

The policeman jerked his head in the direction he had come from. "Let's go to my desk," he said.

Rashad followed Officer Watkins into a large room crowded with desks, file cabinets, and ringing phones. Watkins motioned him toward a chair at the end of the desk. The officer walked around and sank into his own chair.

"Okay," said Officer Watkins, folding his

hands across his ample stomach. "Now what's all this about?"

Rashad started to explain what had happened at the Palace. Before he was finished, Watkins cut him off with a wave of his hand. "This part of the story I know, son," he said. "I've read Officer Bates' report. Save me some time and cut to the chase."

Rashad took a deep breath. He knew this wasn't a good idea, but he decided to risk it. He plunged on with his story.

As Officer Watkins drummed his fingers on the desktop, Rashad tried to explain what had happened. He told the officer how he thought the attack at the Palace was tied in with the man who had approached him on the street the other night. Then he went on to explain that the same man, along with Quincy Martin, had chased him in the van earlier that night. The policeman shook his head.

"Look, kid," he said, not unkindly. "I'm sure your getting mugged was real exciting. You've probably been the hit of your high school all week. But, like I said, I read Officer Bates' report, and it states that you were simply attacked by a homeless person or persons who had moved into that old theater. Not an unusual situation at all."

"But the man on the street . . . " Rashad began.

"From what you've told me, there's no reason to tie that incident into what happened at the Palace," Watkins said, leaning forward. "You know, son, a bump on the head can be a pretty nasty injury. And its effects can last a long time. Personally, I think you went back to school too soon, and your head's doing a number on you— it's making you suspicious of everything and everybody."

"But what about Quincy Martin?" Rashad protested.

"Well, we can talk to him, but we can't hold him long just for hassling you," replied the policeman. "But let's assume for a moment that these guys are after you. What do you think is behind it all?"

Rashad sighed. Oh, boy, here we go, he thought. Feeling very foolish by now, Rashad told Watkins his theory about the old actor.

"What?" Officer Watkins cried.

"I know it sounds crazy," Rashad said, "but I think that old man is trying to get me into that machine. And he's hired Quincy Martin to help him."

"A machine that can make an old guy young again by sucking the life from a kid? Now I *know* your head's doing a number on you," Officer Watkins said.

He leaned back in his chair again. His tone of voice changed. He had been serious and businesslike. Now he sounded fatherly. Rashad was not a crime victim anymore. He was just a boy who maybe had a personal problem. "How are things at school, Rashad?" Officer Watkins asked.

"What's that got to do with anything?" Rashad cried.

"Well, maybe you're carrying too heavy a load, and you probably got a girlfriend taking up your time. I was young once too, you know. It can get pretty stressful." Officer Watkins was smiling now.

"You don't believe anything I've told you, do you?" Rashad demanded.

"Look, I know some strange things have

happened to you, and I wouldn't be surprised if Quincy Martin has been hassling
you. He's been hassling kids for years.
And, yeah, years ago there was a crazy
play at the Palace called *A Deadly
Obsession*. But I don't think it all adds up
to some old psycho chasing you down so
he can get young again. Why don't you go
home, kid, and get some rest?"

Rashad stood up. He felt frustrated and
betrayed. Here he'd thought he was doing
the right thing by reporting his suspicions,
and Officer Watkins was treating him like
a child with an overactive imagination. So
much for serving and protecting, Rashad
thought.

"Come on," Officer Watkins said. "I'll
have one of the officers drive you home."

As much as Rashad resented the idea,
he went along with it. Maybe Quincy was
still hanging around somewhere nearby.

When Rashad got home, his mother
was waiting for him. "Aunt Leslie called,"
she said angrily. "She said you left her
house over an hour ago. Where have you
been? And why did you come home in a
police car?"

"I'm fine, Mom," Rashad said. He didn't want to worry her. "I was just out for some fresh air. That police officer saw me out walking and didn't think I should be out alone at night. So he offered me a ride home."

His mother looked at him suspiciously. "Well, from now on, don't be going out like this without telling anybody where you're going," she ordered. "We were all worried sick about you!"

"I'm sorry, Mom," Rashad said. He went to his room and flopped down on the bed, totally wiped out.

A minute later, Vanessa was standing in his doorway.

"Don't you go giving me any grief, little sister," he said. "I've been through enough tonight."

"I'm not going to give you any grief, Rashad. I've been poking through that folder you brought home from the Palace Theater. I found the letter Spencer Hoover wrote to the director when he was trying to get the lead in that play. It's in his own handwriting. Listen.

"'Dear Mr. Kessler, I am not just an actor who thinks he should get any role he auditions for simply because he has done a few Hollywood movies. It is true that I did some important movies. But Hollywood is more about politics than it is about making great movies. However, I am an honorable man, and I refuse to play their games any longer. As a result, I have been mistreated and will probably never work in Hollywood again.

"But you can help correct this injustice, Mr. Kessler. I very much desire to play Dr. Isaac Hawthorne in your magnificent play, *A Deadly Obsession.* I believe that I am so much like this heroic and tragic figure that I must be the actor who plays him. In a strange and mysterious way, I believe the spirit of Dr. Hawthorne has already entered my soul. I believe you, too, will see this when I audition for the part next week. Sincerely, Spencer Hoover.'"

"Man," Rashad said, "he sounded like he was living in a fantasy world even then."

"Well, his agent is supposed to get back to me tomorrow," Vanessa said. "I called her from a pay phone and left a message on her voice mail." She paused, then went on. "You know, Rashad, I know it sounds cruel, but I hope I find out that Hoover's been dead for years."

"I hope so too," Rashad said, as Vanessa left the room. But I know he's not, he thought. I've seen him—at the Palace Theater, on the street, in the van with Quincy. Maybe he's outside right now staring at our windows.

Rashad picked up the copy of *A Deadly Obsession* he had gotten at the school library. He read the scene again in which the young man dies. He didn't want to, but he felt like he had to.

The stage directions for the scene graphically explained what happened to the young man.

"Hawthorne proceeds to strap the young man into the chair. Then he takes his own place in the other chair, pushes a button, and waits. As the force begins drawing life from Jack Morgan's body, the young man trembles and his muscles contract, causing him to jerk uncontrollably. Slowly his eyes glaze and then gape in rigid death."

Rashad hurled the play across the room. It smashed against the opposite wall, and then fell with a thud onto the floor. In his mind, Rashad could picture the scene—only instead of some unknown actor in the role of Jack Morgan, Rashad saw himself.

6 IN RASHAD'S ENGLISH class the next day, they discussed "David's Kill," the story of a boy's first hunt with his father. As young David and his father relentlessly follow a deer through the forest, the sensitive David grows sick. Despite this, in the end, David brings down the deer.

"Well, what do you have to say about this story?" Mr. Eldridge asked, looking around for volunteers to comment.

"I think it's cool how David bagged the deer and his father didn't," a boy named Noah said. "I liked it that the father thought he was such a hotshot hunter, but his son made the kill."

"I think it was exciting how they kept after the deer, even though they were cold and wet," another student said. "Like they wouldn't give up."

"Rashad, what do you think?" asked Mr. Eldridge.

"I think the story stinks," Rashad said. It

wasn't a comment Mr. Eldridge expected from a student like Rashad.

Mr. Eldridge frowned. "What didn't you like about the story, Rashad?" he asked.

"I hated how they tracked the deer. I mean, it's not fair for people to go into the woods and chase down some poor animal that lives there and isn't bothering anybody. It's not like they need food or anything. That would've been different. The Indians and the pioneers hunted because they had to. And that was okay. But this creep and his son were hunting for the fun of running down some poor creature and killing it." Rashad's words were quick and forceful. His palms were wet. His own strong emotion surprised him.

"Get a grip, man," Franklin muttered from the next desk. "It's only a story."

"Rashad," Mr. Eldridge said, "we aren't here this morning to debate the pros and cons of hunting. We all have different opinions about that. We are trying to discuss elements of the story, such as characterization and plot."

"Well, I hated the whole thing," Rashad declared. "It's a stupid story."

When Rashad had read the story the night before, he found himself identifying with the deer more than with the human characters. He sympathized with the poor, hunted animal, racing through the woods until its heart almost burst with the effort. Rashad *was* that deer the night before when Quincy Martin had been chasing him. He was still that deer, fearing every shadow, waiting for an enemy he didn't even know to strike.

"Hey, man, people are looking at you like you're crazy," Franklin whispered.

Rashad didn't care. "The story glorifies killing for sport."

"Well," Mr. Eldridge said, "perhaps somebody else has a comment more appropriate to our purpose here."

"I thought the story was exciting," a girl said, glancing sideways at Rashad, "but I felt sorry for the deer too. It reminded me of Bambi."

Mr. Eldridge closed his book. "Well, thank you, Mr. Gaines, for squelching our discussion here today. Since our time is almost up, we'll try again tomorrow."

When the bell rang, Rashad and

Franklin walked out of class together. Franklin said, "Man, you want people to think you're freaking or something?"

"If some nut was after you, you'd be freaking too," Rashad said.

"You know, Rash, I've been thinking," said Franklin. "Why don't you go see Mrs. Robinson? She owes you money, right?"

Rashad nodded.

"Well, maybe she can tell you what's gone on there over the years. She's the owner—she should know."

"Not a bad idea, Franklin," Rashad said. "I might just do that. I've got to return her key, anyway."

"Hey, are you going to science club tonight?" Franklin asked.

"Yeah, I guess," said Rashad.

"So am I. See you there." Franklin waved as he headed to his next class.

After school, Mrs. Tyrone bounded into the science club meeting with a huge smile. "Exciting news, everyone. A friend of mine just got back from the Mexican coast where he's been diving with sharks! He made a fantastic movie, and he'll be in our school auditorium tonight to show it.

I'm counting on members of this club to show up in big numbers!"

Rashad was in no mood to watch a shark movie, but he knew he'd have to go. If he hurried, he might have just enough time to make it to Mrs. Robinson's house before the movie.

Rashad drove for about twenty minutes before arriving in an area of upper-class apartments and condominiums.

"Hello, Rashad," Mrs. Robinson greeted him warmly. "What a pleasant surprise. Come in!"

Rashad had worried that she might be angry at him for quitting so quickly, but instead she was gracious and even apologetic.

"Would you like some refreshment, Rashad?" she asked. "A cup of tea? A piece of cake?"

"Thanks, I'll just have a cola," Rashad said. She led him to an elegantly furnished living room where he sat in an overstuffed chair. A few minutes later, the elderly lady came back with cola in a crystal glass.

"Here's your key, Mrs. Robinson," Rashad said, handing it to her. "I feel bad that I couldn't finish the job for you."

Mrs. Robinson quickly raised her hand to silence him. "Rashad, you mustn't feel bad about that," she said. "I'm the one who feels terrible! You could have been seriously hurt or even killed, and it would've been my fault." She shook her head. "I should have never hired another teenager."

"What do you mean, Mrs. Robinson?" Rashad asked.

"Well, there was a terrible tragedy involving a young man I hired to clean up the Palace a few years ago," she said.

Rashad's heart raced. "What happened?" he asked.

"A dreadful accident," Mrs. Robinson explained. "I hired a young man much like you about five years ago. I asked him to clean things up. My dear husband was very ill at the time, and I was handling things. Well, the poor boy died in a freak accident—right on the stage of the theater."

"What kind of accident?" Rashad asked. His mouth went dry. It felt like it was full of chalk dust.

"Oh, my! It was truly horrible. You know, years ago, my husband had the theater converted into a playhouse. Well, when we closed the Palace for good, a lot of the props were still stored there. In fact, the props from the last play stayed right where they were—on the stage.

"We always intended to offer the props to a high school drama department but just never got around to it. You see, my husband was in the last stages of his illness at that time, and things were so hectic.

"Anyway, this young man I hired was cleaning up the stage area. For some reason, he went into one of the props from the last play, a sort of box that was full of wires. He must have played with the switches, and he was electrocuted!"

The room seemed to swim before Rashad's eyes. Maybe Spencer Hoover had been there and had forced the young man into the booth. Then he had pulled the switch!

"How do you know it was an accident?" Rashad asked.

"Why, of course it was! What else could it have been?" Mrs. Robinson seemed alarmed. Rashad didn't want to upset her, so he just went on. "Mrs. Robinson, do you remember the name of the kid who died?"

"Oh, I'll never forget that," Mrs. Robinson said. "You see, we had a major settlement with the family through our attorneys. The boy's name was Damon Marks. Such a waste," she said, shaking her head. "That splendid young man cut down in his prime. Of course, all the wires in the booth were disconnected after that, but I guess the booth is still there."

She reached over and patted Rashad's hand. "I'm so glad you're all right, Rashad. When the police told me that some vagrant had hit you over the head, I was so upset. But before you go, I need to pay you for the work you did."

"To be honest, Mrs. Robinson, I didn't get that much done," Rashad said.

Mrs. Robinson took two one-hundred-dollar bills from her purse and pressed them into Rashad's hand.

"Oh, no, I couldn't take that," Rashad said.

"Nonsense, of course you can," Mrs. Robinson insisted. "It's the least I can do for what you've gone through."

"You're very generous, Mrs. Robinson," Rashad said. "Thanks a lot."

When Rashad and Mrs. Robinson were at the door saying good-bye, the elderly woman again turned serious. "You know, Rashad, I've always had an uneasy feeling about the theater. In the beginning, it was such fun. But then Mr. Kessler staged all those dark little plays—mysteries, horror stories. I've never liked such things."

"Did you ever meet any of the cast from the last play, *A Deadly Obsession?*" Rashad asked.

"Oh, yes," the elderly woman said with a shiver. "I remember the actor who starred in it. Who could forget such a dreadful man! Spencer Hoover was his name. When the play closed, he flew into a murderous rage. He almost choked Mr. Kessler—he had to be pulled off the poor man."

"Did you ever hear what happened to Hoover after the play closed?" Rashad asked.

"No, I didn't," Mrs. Robinson said. "I assumed he'd left the area because I never heard of him again. And that's fine with me. As far as I'm concerned, Spencer Hoover was more of a madman than the character he played!"

7 DISCOURAGED, RASHAD DROVE home. Under any other circumstances, the two hundred dollars in his pocket would have lifted his spirits. But the fact that somebody else had died in that monstrous machine really disturbed him. Rashad realized now that he was not dealing with a guy who *might* commit murder—he was probably dealing with a murderer.

"Rash!" Vanessa cried as Rashad came through the front door. "He's dead!"

"Who?" Rashad demanded.

"Spencer Hoover, silly!" Vanessa yelled, grabbing Rashad's arm. "That means he's not out there looking for you!"

"I don't believe it," Rashad said.

"What's the matter? Can't you stand good news?" Vanessa cried. "Camille Morrison said that Hoover's been dead for years."

"I'm glad if it's true, but . . . "

Vanessa sighed impatiently. "I suppose

now you'll say Hoover's ghost is after you!" she said, shaking her head.

"Tell me what the agent told you," Rashad said.

"Evidently Hoover owed Mrs. Morrison some money. She sent him a bunch of bills trying to collect. Then, a few years ago, she got one back with the message 'Addressee Deceased' scrawled on the envelope."

"That's it?" Rashad asked.

"Well, yeah," Vanessa admitted. "But Mrs. Morrison says she keeps tabs on her former clients, and as far as she could find out, Hoover never worked again after that. No movies, plays, nothing. So she figures he must have died."

Rashad shrugged. It sounded like skimpy evidence to him. Hoover himself could have scrawled that message on the envelope to get the agent off his back. And maybe he'd just never gotten the chance to work in the business again. After all, he had written in that letter to Kessler that he was banned in Hollywood.

After dinner, Rashad drove to school to see the shark movie. Before he left, he put his baseball bat on the front seat beside him—just in case, he told himself. All the way to school, he kept glancing in his rearview mirror to make sure nobody was following him. He drove on well-lit streets as much as possible. When he reached the school parking lot, he sprinted for the door, baseball bat in hand. He saw Summer waiting just inside the school doors.

"Hi, Rashad," she said, looking down at the bat. "Got a game tonight?" she asked, amused.

"No," Rashad said. "Just playing it safe."

"Hey, Vanessa told me about Hoover being dead," Summer said. "Good news for you, huh?"

"Maybe. I'm just not sure I believe it yet," Rashad said.

"Come on, Rashad. You always look on the bad side. Think positive. The guy's out of your hair," Summer said.

"Yeah, right," Rashad answered. I am thinking positively, he thought. I'm *positive* Hoover's still out there.

"Come on," said Summer. "Franklin's saving a couple of seats for us."

The shark movie was spectacular. First, a mid-sized blue shark with a white under-belly came to eat the tuna thrown from a diver's cage. Then more blue sharks gathered, and finally a big pointy-faced mako shark swam up.

"Look," Summer whispered. "That guy is right out there with the sharks, and he's feeding them like they were pet dogs or something!"

"You'd never catch me taking those kinds of chances," Rashad said, fingering the bat propped against his seat.

Everyone applauded after the movie ended. Then, as the lights came on, Rashad heard a hated voice from in back of him.

"Yeah, sharks are real cool. Man, I'd like me a backyard pool full of sharks. I'd invite some dudes I know to swimming parties."

Rashad glanced behind him. "Oh, no," he said to Summer and Franklin. "Quincy Martin's here."

Rashad saw Mrs. Tyrone standing in the aisle, looking coldly at Quincy. "You know very well you have no business here,

Mr. Martin. You don't go to this school any-more, and only students with activity cards can attend school-sponsored functions."

"Awww, teach'," Quincy said mockingly, "you ought to be glad a dropout like me is wanting to attend such a fine cultural event like this one. Who knows? Maybe it'll make me want to come back to school one of these days." He stared directly at Rashad.

"Get lost, creep," Franklin snapped.

Quincy glanced at Franklin and laughed out loud. "Yeah, whatever, man." He looked at Rashad. "Catch you later," he said to Rashad. Then he got up and left the auditorium.

As Rashad, Summer, and Franklin headed to the parking lot, they saw Quincy Martin leaning against the fence around the athletic field, smoking a cigarette. The three would have to pass right by him.

"Ignore him, Rashad," Summer warned.

"I'll try," Rashad said, taking a tighter grip on the baseball bat. The solid wood felt comforting in his hand.

As they passed Quincy, he said in a low, menacing voice, "You make out your last will yet, Gaines?"

Rashad didn't answer.

Quincy flicked his cigarette onto the ground and followed them at a distance. "Don't worry about picking out a coffin, man," he said. "That old dude I'm working with, he's done some tinkering on the box. You know what I mean, Rashad. That's gonna be your coffin."

"Sure was an interesting movie on sharks," Franklin said loudly.

"Yeah, it sure was," agreed Rashad.

"Ignore me while you can, Gaines," Quincy said. "But you're gonna end up in the box. You know it's gonna happen, fool. Maybe it won't be tomorrow or the next day, but one day you're gonna wake up and find yourself in that box. You hear me? Sure you hear me. You got to be thinking about it a lot. You got to be dreaming about it and waking up in cold sweats, man. I can smell fear, Gaines, and you are afraid."

Quincy was getting on Rashad's nerves. This has got to stop, Rashad decided.

Rashad raised the bat in the air and took off after Quincy, yelling, "Get out of my sight, you creep, or I'll bust your head like a rotten pumpkin!"

Quincy spun on his heel and raced off, but his laughter crackled like flames in the darkness long after he was gone.

"Rashad, he's doing a mind game on you," Franklin said.

"Yeah," agreed Summer. "You know Quincy, he's all talk. What could he possibly have to do with what went on at the Palace?"

"I don't know," said Rashad. "But I think I'd better find out before it's too late."

Rashad barely slept that night. Every time he'd fall asleep, a bad dream about Quincy would wake him up. He was still thinking about Quincy and Hoover the next morning as he walked into the kitchen to grab a banana for the trip to school.

"Good morning, son." His mother patted him on the shoulder as he moved by her. "Sleep well?"

"Yeah, I slept okay," he replied.

"Good. Now Rashad, you need to be home by 5:30 tonight. We have an appointment with a man who called last evening after you were in bed. This man—Mr. Finch, I think—is offering a scholarship to a student who is good in science. Apparently, he's some kind of chemist who went to East High, and he wants students from his old school to be successful. He's coming to talk to us about your plans for college. Isn't that exciting?"

The last thing Rashad wanted to think about right now was college. He was more concerned about the next few days than he was about next fall. But he answered, "Okay, Mom. I won't forget," to end the conversation and get to school.

When Rashad got to school, it was as though his nightmares had come true. Quincy Martin was waiting for him by his locker. "Yo! Gaines!" Quincy said. He had several textbooks under his arm. "I'm back in school. Heartwarming, huh? I start today."

"That's impossible. You dropped out in tenth grade!" Rashad cried. He could smell the disgusting odor of cigarettes that hung around Quincy like a fog.

"Well, I'm back. And I'm officially a sophomore—again. So I probably won't be in any of your classes, but we'll meet in the halls a lot."

"I'm thrilled," Rashad said.

"I thought you might be," Quincy replied. "And maybe some afternoon when no one's looking, I'll get the chance to stuff you into my van and deliver you to the box like the man wants." He leered at Rashad.

"You threaten me around here, and I'll turn you in," Rashad warned.

"Yeah, well, give it your best shot, Gaines. I had a long talk with our kind-hearted principal, and I got her believing I'm here to turn my life around. I almost had her crying, man. She's on a 'save the poor juvenile' kick, so I doubt that she'll believe you." Quincy laughed and sauntered off down the hall.

Rashad turned sharply and headed for the principal's office. But then he thought about it. Quincy was probably right. Teachers and principals had good hearts. They didn't *want* to punish children. They wanted to help them. They wanted to believe that troublemakers like Quincy were just lonely and neglected children who needed help. Rashad's claims that Quincy was threatening him would probably go unheeded, at least for now—until Quincy was given a chance to "prove himself." But Rashad knew that by then it might be too late. Nevertheless, he decided not to talk to the principal yet.

Rashad had a few stops to make after school. When he finally got home around 5:30, his parents were having coffee with a man in a dark suit. The stranger sat on the couch with his back to Rashad.

"Oh, Rashad," Mrs. Gaines said as she stood up. "We've just been talking about you. Come meet Mr. Finch."

Mr. Gaines, who was also seated on the couch, turned toward Rashad and grinned proudly. "Mr. Finch is quite impressed with your grade point," he said.

The visitor turned slowly, and Rashad went rigid. The narrow shoulders. The squarish jaw. The haunting, glittering eyes.

It was the man who had asked directions to the deli. The man in the van with Quincy. The man stalking Rashad—in Rashad's house, talking to Rashad's parents!

8 "ALLOW ME TO introduce myself," the man said in a fine, strong voice. "I'm Thomas Finch." Smiling broadly, he extended his hand toward Rashad.

Rashad shook his head. "No," he said slowly. "I know you. I've seen you before!"

"Excuse me?" the man said, apparently confused. "I haven't lived in this city for years."

"That's not true!" said Rashad. "You were in the van that night with Quincy Martin. I saw your face when you lit your cigarette."

"Rashad!" Mrs. Gaines cried, shocked at her son's behavior. "What's the matter with you, son? Don't you feel well?"

"This man has gone to a great deal of trouble to come here tonight," Mr. Gaines said sternly.

"His name isn't Thomas Finch," Rashad insisted. "It's Spencer Hoover." He was sure of it. The eyes were the same ones he'd seen on the poster for *A Deadly Obsession.*

Mr. Finch stood, smiling faintly. "Perhaps I'd better leave. This young man is clearly not well."

"Mr. Finch," Mr. Gaines said, rising from the couch. "I'm really very sorry. My son is never like this."

Mrs. Gaines shook her head. "He must have a fever or something," she said.

"I'll see you to the door, Mr. Finch," Rashad's father offered, throwing an icy stare his son's way.

Mr. Gaines escorted the man out and came back into the living room.

"Rashad!" he cried. "What in the world's going on with you? That man was offering a four-year scholarship to the state university!"

"That's a lie," Rashad said. "He's an actor. He's playing a role so he can get into this house. He's already killed two guys, and now he wants to kill me!"

"Good Lord!" Mrs. Gaines gasped. "How can you say such a thing?"

Rashad came closer to his mother. "Mom, you said you saw a play at the

Palace a long time ago—*A Deadly Obsession*. You said you sensed evil in the theater during the play. And you said the actor was really weird. Well, that was him, Mom. That wasn't Thomas Finch. That guy's name is Spencer Hoover. Didn't you recognize him?"

"That's ridiculous, and you know it, Rashad," Mrs. Gaines said. "That play was years ago, and Mr. Finch had nothing to do with it."

"Rashad, I have to say that I'm appalled at your behavior," said Mr. Gaines.

It was obvious to Rashad that neither of his parents was going to believe him. There was no sense taking it any further.

"I'm sorry," Rashad said. He turned and went to his room.

* * *

Rashad went to the school library early the next morning. The man who pretended to be Thomas Finch claimed he had once attended East High. Rashad located the old yearbook section of the library and began his search.

It took a while, but Rashad finally

spotted Thomas Finch in a yearbook from the early 1960s. He was a skinny boy with glasses.

Rashad went to the librarian. "You've been here a while, haven't you, Ms. Wallace?" he asked.

"Oh, yes," the older woman replied, "almost thirty years."

"So you probably remember a lot of the students who've gone here, right?" Rashad continued.

"Well, my memory's not as good as it used to be, but I still remember many of them," Ms. Wallace said.

Rashad held the yearbook page out for her to see. "Do you know what became of this guy, Thomas Finch?"

Ms. Wallace smiled. "Oh, yes. He was very bright. He became a chemist and won all sorts of awards."

"Where is he now?" Rashad asked.

"He died in Vietnam," Ms. Wallace explained. "He was killed in a helicopter crash during the war."

I knew it! Rashad said to himself. I knew it wasn't Thomas Finch who came to my house to offer me a scholarship. It was Hoover looking for a way to get to me.

During lunch, Rashad told Franklin what had happened.

"Hoover was in my living room sweet-talking my parents with some lies about a scholarship—and they believed him! When I freaked, they got furious!"

"Tell your folks about Finch being dead," Franklin urged. "They've got to believe you then."

"I don't think so," Rashad muttered. "They both think I've lost my mind."

He looked up to see Quincy Martin approaching.

"Oh, man!" he groaned. "Just what I need—that big baboon bothering me."

"You look a little stressed out, Gaines," Quincy said with mock concern. "What's the matter? Aren't you getting enough sleep?"

Rashad ignored his questions. "Just out of curiosity, Martin," he said, "what are you getting out of working for the old actor? What's in it for you to get mixed up in murder and end up on death row?"

"Well, let's just put it this way," Quincy

said. "By next month at this time, I'll be driving a brand new car. And I'll have money in my pockets and a good-looking lady on my arm. And you'll be pushing up daisies, hear me?"

Rashad tried to keep his cool. "Quincy, do you really think that crazy old actor has any money? He's stringing you along. He's a liar and a con man. After you do his dirty work, he'll kill you too," Rashad said.

"You don't know what you're talkin' about, man," Quincy said. "That man used to be a Hollywood actor. He made tons of money, and he stashed it all away."

"He was a bit-part movie actor who made pennies, Martin," Rashad said.

Quincy shook his head. "You believe what you want, Gaines," he said. "I'm just sorry you won't be around for me to prove it to you." He pointed a beefy finger at Rashad. *"Catch you* later," he said, laughing. Then he turned and strolled away. What a creep, Rashad thought.

After school, Rashad and Franklin headed toward the parking lot. As they approached Rashad's car, Rashad put his hand on Franklin's shoulder. "Wait!"

Rashad said. "Who's that leaning on my car?"

Franklin squinted his eyes and peered ahead. "I don't know," he said. "Looks like some old guy."

"It's him, Franklin!" Rashad said. "It's Hoover!"

"Is your baseball bat in your car?" Franklin asked.

"Yeah, but a lot of good that'll do me now," answered Rashad. "He's leaning on the door." He glanced around at the dozens of students heading toward their cars. "Maybe he won't try anything with all these people around."

The man had his head turned in the other direction, seemingly deep in thought. Rashad and Franklin approached cautiously and stopped a few feet from the car.

"What are you doing here?" Rashad asked in what he hoped was a threatening voice.

The man turned his head slowly and smiled.

"Rashad," he said in a deep, velvety voice. "I must speak with you." His voice reminded Rashad of Vincent Price, the actor who starred in lots of horror movies years ago. He, too, had a deep, emotional voice—but he was scary, just the same.

"Stay away from me, Hoover," Rashad warned.

"Tsk, tsk, my boy," said Hoover. "You have the wrong opinion of me." Rashad noticed that the man had not denied being Hoover.

"Yeah, right," Rashad said bitterly. "You're that bighearted businessman, Thomas Finch, who wants to give me a scholarship. Only problem with that is Thomas Finch has been dead for a long time!"

"My, you're clever, aren't you?" Hoover said with obvious admiration. "It was unfortunate that I had to lie about that. I simply wanted the chance to talk to you in a reasonable way."

"Quit beating around the bush, Hoover," Franklin said. "What do you want with Rashad?"

Hoover regarded Franklin for a brief second, as if it was the first time he'd noticed the boy's presence. Then he turned his full attention back to Rashad. "First of all, I'm not some monster who plans some ghastly experiment to recover my youth," Hoover began. "I played a demented scientist in a play once, true, but I'm not a madman."

"Okay, so you're not a madman," Rashad snapped. *"What do you want?"*

Hoover held up his hand. "All in good time, my boy, all in good time," he said in a soothing tone. "For some time, I've been searching for a talented young man—one who has the look of an actor, a youthful, robust young man." His eyes flickered intensely as he spoke. "Sadly, I'm getting along in years, and I wish to be a mentor to such a person so that my own great skills do not perish with me. I'll admit I've had to use some rather unusual means to discover the youth I wish to take under my wing. But my search has not proved fruitless in that it has led me to you, Rashad. Truly, all I seek is someone to carry on my acting legacy."

Rashad shook his head. "You're a liar, man," he said. "You killed Damon Marks! What about that? He died in that machine of yours."

Hoover began to tremble, his long, thin fingers fluttering. "An accident, a dreadful accident. There was a short in the wiring . . . the boy perished . . . I fled . . . I was afraid the police wouldn't understand."

"You're a murderer, Spencer Hoover!" Rashad cried. "You killed Damon Marks, and now you want to kill me!"

Spencer Hoover suddenly smiled and said, "'An honorable murderer, if you will; for naught I did in hate, but all in honor.' *Othello*, fifth act, I believe." Then he wrapped himself in his thin coat and hurried away.

9 "SHOULD I GRAB the guy while you call the cops?" Franklin asked, starting after Hoover.

"No," Rashad replied. "What would they arrest him for? Quoting Shakespeare?"

A fine sheen of perspiration had broken out on Rashad's face. Now he shivered in the cool wind.

"Did you see those eyes?" he asked Franklin.

"Yeah, man. Weird," his friend said. "Hey, let's follow him at a distance and see where he goes."

"Good idea," said Rashad as they both climbed into his car. "Let's give him a couple of minutes' head start, though, so he doesn't spot us."

Hoover walked along quickly, never looking back. The boys followed at a safe distance. When the actor got to the corner of one street, he took a sharp turn. For a moment he was shielded from sight by a tall hedge. When the boys reached the corner, Hoover was gone.

"Oh, man, where'd he go?" cried Rashad.

"He could've gone into any one of those crummy hotels," Franklin said. "Or maybe he caught a bus somewhere."

"You know, it's funny," remarked Rashad, "but since I met Hoover and talked with him, he doesn't seem quite so intimidating. He's just a skinny, wasted old man with weird eyes and a big voice."

"Yeah, well, that might be," Franklin replied. "But remember, he's got Quincy Martin working for him. And there's nothing skinny and wasted about him."

* * *

Rashad found Summer later on, and they went out for an ice-cream cone. Rashad hadn't felt like doing that in a long time.

"You should've seen the little creep," Rashad said. "I was expecting some kind of powerful guy, but there's nothing big about him but his voice. I felt kind of like Dorothy in *The Wizard of Oz*. You know, when she finds out the big scary wizard is just a wimp behind a curtain."

Summer smiled. "I'm glad you're feeling better, Rash. But I still want you to be careful," she said.

"Oh, I'll be careful all right. But I'm not going to let this spook me so much that it interferes with my social life," Rashad said, smiling at her.

"Hey, I'm all for that!" Summer said, smiling back.

When Rashad got home, his father wasn't home yet, and his mother was putting the finishing touches on dinner.

"Mr. Finch called," Rashad's mother said, obviously thrilled. "He said he understood that teenagers have moods. He's willing to forget what happened and interview you again for the scholarship. Isn't that wonderful?"

Rashad sighed. "Mom, look," he said. "I don't want to upset you, but the guy is a fake."

"Never mind, Rashad," his mother answered. "We'll talk about it at dinner when your father's home. Look, I've made your favorite meal—steak and baked potatoes. And we've got a special dessert—chocolate cheesecake."

She doesn't believe me because she doesn't want to, Rashad thought. She and Dad need all the help they can get to send me to college, and they want the best for me.

"Where's Nessa?" Rashad asked, noticing that his mother had only three steaks out.

"At Julie's house working on their project for social studies," Mrs. Gaines replied. "She won't be home for dinner."

When Mr. Gaines came home, the three sat down to dinner.

"Poor Vanessa, missing this meal," Rashad said.

"We'll save her a piece of cheesecake," Mrs. Gaines said.

The family talked casually for most of the meal. Rashad told them about the shark movie and the science club.

"Speaking of science, Rashad," his father said, pushing his empty plate aside, "did your mother tell you that Mr. Finch called and he's willing to give you another chance?"

"Yeah, she told me, Dad. But do we have to talk about it now?" Rashad asked.

"Son, he's talking about a scholarship worth maybe *twenty thousand dollars*," Mr. Gaines answered. "Yes, we *do* have to talk about it now."

"Mr. Finch says he's talked to your counselor and some of your teachers," added Mrs. Gaines. "He's satisfied that you're one of the best East High has to offer. Now, he didn't want to promise anything, but he indicated that you might be a shoo-in for that scholarship. Anyone for dessert?" she added, getting up from the table.

"Please," said Mr. Gaines. "That cheesecake looks great."

"Me too, Mom," said Rashad.

Mrs. Gaines came back from the kitchen with three plates. "Here you go," she said, placing a plate in front of each of them.

Mr. Gaines took a bite. "Hmm, this is so good," he said.

"No kidding," agreed Rashad. It was so rich, so chocolatey.

"Back to the scholarship, Rashad," his father continued. "Can we give it one more try with Mr. Finch? He said he could come later tonight."

Rashad took his last bite and sighed. "Dad," he began, but he stopped when he saw his father put his hand to his head.

"Whew," Mr. Gaines said. "I must have eaten too fast. I'm a little dizzy."

"What's wrong, Dad?" Rashad asked. He glanced at his mother. She, too, had stopped eating and was holding her head. "Mom?" he asked anxiously. "What's the matter?"

"I'm . . . so lightheaded," she said, her voice barely above a whisper. "I'm afraid I can't finish this cheesecake Mr. Finch . . . sent us."

"Mr. Finch sent us this?" Rashad cried, standing up. Suddenly he realized his legs were wobbly. He sank back into the chair. The room seemed to be spinning, and he could hear a ringing in his ears. A bolt of terror went through him. What if the cheesecake was poisoned? No, he thought, Hoover doesn't want to kill me. He just wants to be able to get to me without interference from anyone else. He looked with alarm at his parents. Both had passed out where they sat, their heads down on the table and their arms limp at their sides.

Rashad stumbled from his chair. "Got to call 911 for help," he said aloud. "911 . . . " His legs felt like putty. He dropped to his knees halfway to the phone. The room was spinning like a top. He knew he had only a few seconds of consciousness left. It all depended on him. If he didn't get help, no one would come. And Hoover would get him.

He dragged himself across the floor, fighting against the drowsiness that numbed him. His sight was blurring, and his arms wouldn't hold his weight any longer. He grabbed for the end table that held the phone. Slowly, his hands inched up the leg and onto the top of the table. He snatched the phone and pushed 911. But as he held the receiver to his ear, he realized that the phone was dead. Someone had cut the wires.

Rashad hit the rug face down. Unable to move, he lay there on the verge of passing out. Suddenly he heard a crash and a tinkle of glass. Through the fog in his head, he recognized the sound of the front door's bolt being pulled back. A few seconds later, he felt cool air sweep over his body as the door opened. Then he heard heavy footsteps coming toward him. Suddenly he was aware of hands grabbing him roughly by the shoulders and rolling him onto his back. With a supreme effort, Rashad opened his eyes.

Quincy Martin loomed over him. "Caught ya!" he said, smiling down on Rashad.

Spencer Hoover moved slowly into view. He looked gray and fuzzy to Rashad's fading sight. His voice sounded as if it were very far away.

"So, my boy, we meet again," Rashad heard the actor say. "And this time, on better terms—at least for me. I'm so sorry about your parents, Rashad, but they'll be fine. By the time they come to, you'll be gone—long gone!"

The room was turning dark. Rashad was losing consciousness so fast that Hoover disappeared from his sight. The last thing he heard was Quincy Martin saying, "He's out colder than a fish on ice, Mr. Hoover." Then everything went black.

* * *

Rashad knew he was coming out of something, that he was slowly regaining consciousness. Yet each time he got close to waking up, his mind seemed to retreat into darkness. It was as if his mind were wrapped in layer after layer of sticky cobwebs, and his thoughts just couldn't quite break through. But slowly, one sense at a time, Rashad came to.

He was aware that he was in a standing position and that something hard and rough was pressing against his back. At the same time, he realized that the air around him had a familiar musty smell. And from somewhere nearby, he detected the faint odor of a burning cigarette.

Rashad's mouth was dry. He moved his tongue and swallowed. He tasted stale chocolate followed by a faint bitter flavor. His eyelids seemed to be welded shut, and for a few more seconds, he avoided the effort of opening them. In fact, he was tempted to retreat into the darkness inside his head again when someone coughed. He opened his eyes slightly and was immediately sorry.

"So," Quincy Martin said, "Sleeping

Beauty's awake!"

Rashad groaned. Quincy? What was he doing here? Rashad tried to think, but the fog hadn't quite lifted from his brain. He vaguely remembered dinner, and the delicious steak his mother had served. And then he remembered the cheesecake and his parents passed out at the table. He saw himself crawling desperately toward the phone. The cake! It must have been drugged! That was the bitter taste in his mouth.

Rashad opened his eyes all the way. His eyes burned, and he instinctively tried to rub them clear with the back of his hand. But for some reason his hand wouldn't move. Slowly his vision cleared. He was on the stage of the Palace Theater. He was standing against the picket fence prop he had seen earlier. His ankles were bound together, and his hands were tied to large bolts that had been screwed into the fence. He tried to pull one wrist loose, but the knots were too tight.

"Don't bother," Quincy sneered. He stuck his face next to Rashad's. Rashad reeled from the smell of cigarettes. "How's your stress level now, Gaines? Feeling a little anxious, are ya?"

Now Rashad could see the booth looming in the middle of the stage. He fought to stay calm. "Look, Quincy," he said, "you don't have to do this. Let me go, and I promise I won't say anything about your involvement in all of this."

"Involvement in what, pray tell?" Rashad heard the rich, rolling voice of Hoover behind him. "By the time we've finished, all evidence will be gone. All that will be left behind will be a young man, a dashing young man, I dare say. One who's headed for stardom—again! Only this time, he will not fail!"

A sense of horror overwhelmed Rashad, a numb despair. They had him. They had won. Now it was only a matter of time.

Hoover noticed the fear in Rashad's eyes. He looked sad. "I'm sorry it had to come to this, my boy, truly I am. But I have no choice. I am growing old and, worse yet, I am ill. Do you understand? The doctors have given me less than six months to live. I have no choice but to reverse the aging process. If I don't, all the roles I am destined to play will go unfulfilled. Besides, think of it not as dying but as becoming immortal—through me!"

Rashad laughed scornfully. "The only thing I'm going to become is a corpse," he said. "I read the play. You think you can use some kind of machine to suck the life force out of my body and become young again. Well, you can't. It doesn't take a rocket scientist to figure out that a crazy plan like that won't work."

"It will work!" Hoover hissed, his eyes blazing. "We are all nothing but electrical impulses! Electrical impulses can be moved from one machine to another. We are all, in a sense, electrical machines!"

"What about Damon Marks?" Rashad reminded the actor. "I guess his electrical impulses must have backfired, right?"

"That was an error," Hoover said. "I have corrected it. Besides, the Marks boy was weak. He didn't have your strength of character, your inner fire. He walked into my trap like a lamb. You, on the other hand, have fought me like a lion. But I will control your strength and use it to make my experiment work." He smiled dreamily. "When I am young and healthy again, I will rule the world of theater. I will become a second Olivier, another Barrymore! It can happen! It *will* happen! And you will share in my triumphs. You will supply the energy that powers the world's greatest actor!"

Rashad stared at him in disbelief. It was obvious that Hoover was totally insane. He truly believed his own mad ideas.

Rashad tried again. "Look, man," he said, "we all grow old and we die. You can't stop that. But I'm telling you, there's no way for an old man to get young again in this world!"

"Silence!" Hoover shrieked, some of the color draining from his sunken cheeks. "It's time to begin. Quincy! Prepare the machine!"

Rashad sagged against the fence. His arms ached from being tied up so high, but that was the least of his worries. He knew that Hoover would carry out his mad scheme. It might kill both of them, but that was no comfort. For the first time, Rashad truly realized that he might die. He thought about his parents and Vanessa. They'd never know what happened to him. He wouldn't be around to see Vanessa go out on her first date or graduate from high school. And he'd never go to college. Worst of all, he wouldn't have a chance to build a life with Summer. Rashad blinked back tears.

Hoover stood over Quincy at the booth giving him instructions. The actor was smiling like a grinning skeleton, so tightly was his papery skin stretched over his facial bones. He turned to Rashad. "Now listen carefully, my boy," he said. "I will sit in this chair beside the booth, and you will sit here." He pointed to the chair inside the booth. "See how the wires lead from one chair to the other? As the electrical current is reversed, the life force shall travel from your body to mine. As you grow weak, I shall grow strong!"

"No, it's crazy! It can't happen!" Rashad said desperately. While Quincy and Hoover fiddled with the wires, Rashad strained against the ropes. He thrashed around for a few seconds, but it was hopeless. The ropes were just too strong. He stood panting, sweat glistening on his forehead. There had to be a way out of this. There just had to be.

Then it came to him. Quincy would have to untie him in order to get him to the chair. Quincy was big, but it was mostly flab. He smoked a lot, and he wasn't in very good shape. Rashad, on the other hand, worked out with weights and ran several miles each week. Maybe, just maybe, he could overpower Quincy. It was worth a try.

Rashad stood quietly, conserving his strength. He looked at the booth. It was glowing with an eerie light. It was as if the evil of Spencer Hoover had entered it, giving it an unearthly glow.

10

HOOVER SEATED HIM-
SELF in the chair beside
the booth and strapped
himself in. Like a king on his throne, he
regarded Quincy and Rashad. "It is time,"
he announced, his voice echoing through-
out the auditorium. "Escort the sacrifice
to the Chair of Immortality."

Quincy strutted over to Rashad. "That's
you," he said, reaching up to untie
Rashad's hands. "Now, we're going to
walk over, and you're going into the box.
You give me any trouble, and I'll kick your
teeth in, whether that old fool likes it or
not. Understand?" It was obvious that
Quincy knew the experiment was a farce.
He was only interested in the money he
expected to get when Rashad was dead.

Rashad looked steadily at him. "Yeah, I
understand," he said quietly.

Spencer Hoover frowned. "There's no
need for crude threats, Quincy," he said.
"Certainly by now Rashad understands

what an honor this is. Let us proceed." He sat back and closed his eyes. Rashad noticed that he gripped the arms of his chair as if he could already feel energy coursing through them.

"Sure thing, Mr. H," Quincy said. "Whatever you say." He finished untying Rashad's hands. Then he grabbed him by the collar. "Come on. You've got a reserved seat over here."

Slowly, the two boys crossed the stage. It was difficult for Rashad to walk with his ankles bound. He could feel Quincy's cold, meaty hand still gripping his neck. Then Quincy loosened his hand and shoved Rashad.

"Okay, fool, get in there," he said.

Rashad nodded and bent his head as if he were about to enter the booth. It's now or never, he thought. Suddenly he whirled around and grabbed Quincy in a headlock. Then, with all his might, he threw Quincy toward the opening of the booth. Quincy gagged and flailed his arms, but it was no use. He flew head first into the chair that awaited Rashad. A surge of voltage flooded the booth, and Quincy's body twitched violently and gave off a fiery glow. Then Quincy Martin was still.

"Fool!" Rashad heard Spencer Hoover shriek. He looked at the old actor. His mouth was a gaping hole, and all color had drained from his face. His eyes were frozen open in horror at the jolt of lightning that was tearing through his body. Smoke smothered his dying curses.

Rashad gagged and backed away from the box. Red and yellow flames leaped over the wires around Quincy and began to roar and crackle as they found the dry wood of the booth.

Rashad had to get out of there fast. Forgetting that his ankles were still bound, he turned to run, but the bindings tripped him up, and he fell to the floor of the stage. He tried to loosen the bindings, but Rashad was not familiar with the knots Quincy had used, and he gave up.

Smoke began to gather, acrid smoke that burned Rashad's eyes and nostrils. He noticed that flames were licking at the curtains that surrounded the stage. The entire stage would be a roaring inferno in a matter of minutes. He would have to go through the auditorium.

Rashad half rolled, half crawled down the steps leading off the stage. He clawed his way up the carpeted aisle. His arms began to ache, and his ankles burned from the tight bindings. Sweat poured down his body, drenching him. He could hear the crackling, popping sounds of the fire behind him.

Desperately, Rashad pulled himself toward the double doors. The smoke was thick and choking now. Glancing back, he saw that the entire stage was ablaze. In the center, the glass box was a solid sheet of flame.

Rashad reached the double doors. He threw his weight against them and fell through into the lobby. It was easier to breathe now, but he knew he was still in danger. Gritting his teeth, he dragged himself toward the front door. The pain in his ankles was almost unbearable now. Suddenly, the big double doors burst open, and Rashad saw the hands of a policeman reaching down for him. It was the last thing he saw before passing out.

* * *

When Rashad woke up, he was flat on his back. His father was bending over him. He smiled when he saw Rashad's eyes open.

"Dad?" Rashad croaked. His throat felt like it was on fire.

"It's okay," Mr. Gaines said. "You're safe now, son. You're in the hospital." Rashad could hear the relief in his father's voice.

"I am?" Rashad asked, his head still fuzzy. He tried to swallow but began coughing instead. The pain in his chest was so great that he was sure his lungs were collapsing.

"You're suffering from smoke inhalation, Rashad. That's why your throat is so sore."

"Mom? Where's Mom?" Rashad whispered hoarsely.

"She's right down the hall. That cheesecake Finch—no, I guess it's Hoover, isn't it?— sent us was drugged," his father said. "It made us all pretty sick, but luckily Vanessa came home. She found your mother and me and called the police from the neighbors' house. That's how they found you. Vanessa was sure Hoover had taken you to the Palace.

"Anyway, your mom had a reaction to the drug, but she's going to be okay. In fact, she's going to be released tomorrow." He sat down next to Rashad. "You've been out cold since they brought you in last night."

Rashad remembered where he'd been. "The Palace! Did it burn?"

His dad nodded. "To the ground," he said. "The firemen are still sifting through the rubble. Can you tell me what happened, son?"

Rashad told his father all about the glass box, Quincy, and Hoover.

"So when the stage caught on fire, I escaped," he concluded. "I made it to the lobby, and then I looked up and saw a policeman. That's all I remember."

Mr. Gaines shook his head sadly. "And to think your mother and I didn't believe you," he said. "I'm so sorry."

"It's all right, Dad," Rashad whispered. "I had a hard time believing it myself, and it was happening to me! It's like the whole thing was a bad dream."

"Well, you're here with us now. That's the important thing," said his father. "I'm going to go tell your mother you're awake. She'll want to come see you."

As his father opened the door to leave, Vanessa came bounding in.

"Big brother!" she yelled. She flung herself onto the bed and gave Rashad a hug.

"Hey, go easy, Nessa," Rashad whispered. "I'm wounded in action, you know."

"How do you feel?" Vanessa asked.

"Not too bad," said Rashad. "My throat's a little sore is all. Hey, thanks for saving my life, little sister."

Vanessa smiled. "No problem," she said. Then she winked. "But you owe me now, you know."

"Tell you what," Rashad said, smiling slyly. "We've got some great chocolate cheesecake at home. I'll dish you up a piece when I get home. How does that sound?"

"No way!" said Vanessa, laughing. She reached out and punched him playfully in the arm.

Even though it hurt, Rashad laughed. He was alive. He could build a life with Summer, and he'd be there to see Vanessa grow up. And she was one cool little sister!